THE THREE MUSKETEERS

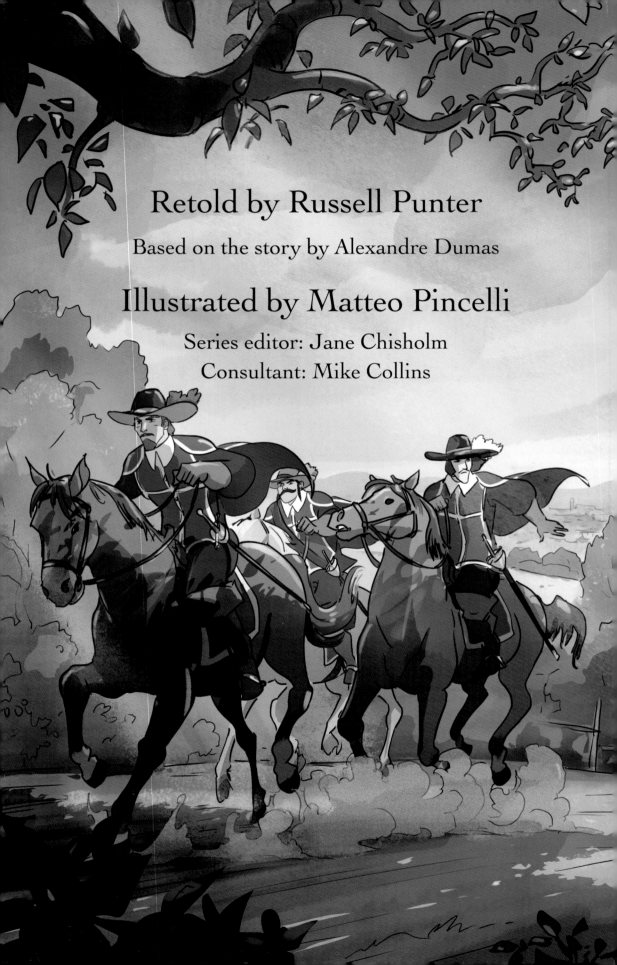

Retold by Russell Punter

Based on the story by Alexandre Dumas

Illustrated by Matteo Pincelli

Series editor: Jane Chisholm
Consultant: Mike Collins

THE THREE MUSKETEERS

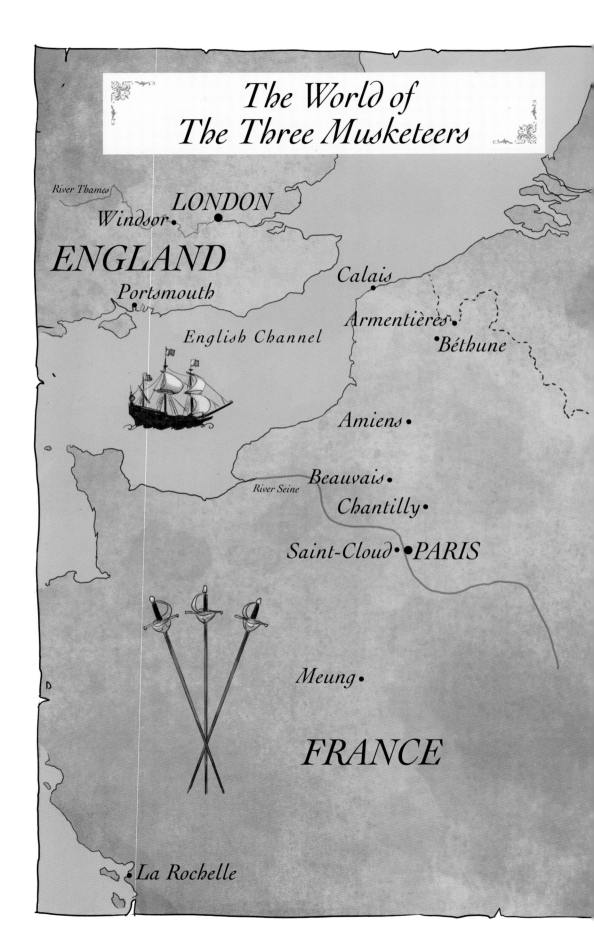

The World of The Three Musketeers

River Thames

LONDON

Windsor

ENGLAND

Portsmouth

Calais

Armentières

Béthune

English Channel

Amiens

Beauvais

River Seine

Chantilly

Saint-Cloud ••PARIS

Meung

FRANCE

La Rochelle

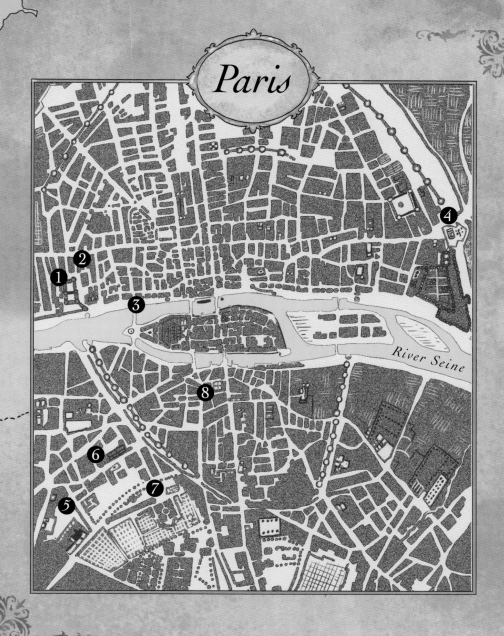

Paris

1 - Louvre Palace

2 - Cardinal's Palace

3 - Pont Neuf

4 - Bastille Prison

5 - Convent of the Carmes-Déschaux

6 - Monsieur de Tréville's mansion

7 - Luxembourg Gardens

8 - Rue de la Harpe

France, 1626.
The land is ruled by King Louis XIII, alongside his advisor, the power-hungry Cardinal Richelieu.

Eighteen-year-old d'Artagnan is on his way to Paris to join the king's guards, captained by Monsieur de Tréville.

But as the proud young man arrives at the market town of Meung one afternoon, it's his elderly horse that attracts the locals' attention...

JUST LOOK AT THE **STATE** OF THAT MAN'S **HORSE!**

I'M SURPRISED IT CAN **WALK!**

WHEN THE MAN TURNS HIS BACK...

TURN AND **FACE** ME, MR. **SNIDE!**

INSULTED, THE MAN DRAWS HIS SWORD...

BUT BEFORE HE CAN STRIKE D'ARTAGNAN, THE MAN'S TWO ASSOCIATES LAUNCH AN ATTACK ON HIS BEHALF...

WHACK!

AGH!

OOF!

ARGH!

SMACK!

THUMP!

THE 'INSOLENT BOY' IS *HERE* AND READY TO **CONTINUE** WHERE HE **LEFT OFF**!

I ASSUME YOU WON'T **RUN AWAY** IN FRONT OF A LADY?

WHY YOU...

THINK*!*

EVEN A *SLIGHT* DELAY COULD RUIN **EVERYTHING**!

YOU'RE **RIGHT**, MILADY.

YOU GO **YOUR** WAY, AND I'LL GO **MINE**!

THE MAN AND MILADY SPEED OFF IN OPPOSITE DIRECTIONS...

YOU **COWARD***!* YOU **VILLAIN***!*

HO, THERE*!* WHAT ABOUT YOUR **BILL**, SIR?

OW! MY RIBS FEEL LIKE A HORSE HAS GALLOPED OVER THEM!

WHO *WAS* THAT ROGUE?

HE NEVER GAVE HIS **NAME!** WHO WAS THAT **WOMAN?**

HE CALLED HER **'MILADY'.** JUDGING BY HER **ACCENT,** SHE'S **ENGLISH.**

FOLLOWING A FEW DAYS SPENT AT THE INN, RECOVERING FROM HIS WOUNDS, D'ARTAGNAN TRAVELS TO PARIS...

AFTER HE'S SOLD HIS OLD HORSE...

...AND BOUGHT A NEW SWORD...

...HE MAKES HIS WAY TO THE MANSION OF MONSIEUR DE TRÉVILLE, CAPTAIN OF THE MUSKETEERS...

NOW, YOU TWO, I DINED WITH HIS MAJESTY THE KING AND **CARDINAL RICHELIEU** LAST NIGHT...

...THE CARDINAL TOLD ME THAT THE PREVIOUS EVENING **HIS** GUARDS **ARRESTED** THREE OF **MY** MUSKETEERS FOR **CAROUSING** IN A LOCAL TAVERN!

THERE FOLLOWED A **SWORD FIGHT**, AFTER WHICH THESE MUSKETEERS **FLED**...

THE **SHAME** OF IT! HIS MAJESTY'S MUSKETEERS **ARRESTED**, THEN **DEFEATED** BY THE CARDINAL'S GUARDS!

ALL THREE OF YOU WERE RECOGNIZED... WHERE *IS* **ATHOS,** BY THE WAY?

WOUNDED, SIR! BUT HE PUT UP A **GOOD** FIGHT!

AT THAT MOMENT...

ATHOS!

HANG IT, CAPTAIN, YOU CAN'T WIN **EVERY** BATTLE!

YOU SENT FOR ME, MONSIEUR DE TRÉVILLE?

IT IS *I* WHO SHOULD APOLOGIZE TO *YOU* FOR MY **LATE ARRIVAL,** CAPTAIN. I WAS **ASSAULTED** BY A **ROGUE** AT MEUNG, WHICH **DELAYED** ME BY SEVERAL DAYS...

AFTER D'ARTAGNAN HAS TOLD THE TALE...

THIS **MAN** WHO WAS TALKING WITH THE **ENGLISH LADY** – DID HE HAVE A **SCAR** ON HIS **FOREHEAD?**

WHY **YES!** IT LOOKED LIKE A **BULLET GRAZE.**

HIS NAME IS **ROCHEFORT.** THE **CARDINAL** USES MEN LIKE HIM TO KEEP HIMSELF IN **POWER.**

I URGE YOU TO **STEER CLEAR OF** HIM!

WHY WAS A **CARDINAL'S** MAN CONSPIRING WITH AN **ENGLISHWOMAN?** WE'RE ON THE VERGE OF **WAR** WITH **HER COUNTRY!**

DON'T **WORRY.** THE CARDINAL ALWAYS ACTS IN THE **INTERESTS** OF **FRANCE,** SO THAT HE CAN REMAIN IN **POWER.**

BUT HE DOESN'T CARE WHO GETS **HURT** IN THE PROCESS, BE THEY ENGLISH **OR** FRENCH. SO BE **WARNED!**

NOW THEN, YOU'VE COME TO JOIN THE **KING'S GUARD...**

YES, MONSIEUR.

FIRST YOU MUST JOIN **MONSIEUR DES ESSART'S** COMPANY...

THERE YOU'LL LEARN HORSEMANSHIP AND FENCING. **PROVE** YOURSELF **WORTHY** AND YOU'LL BE A KING'S **MUSKETEER** ONE DAY!

AS DE TRÉVILLE PREPARES D'ARTAGNAN'S PAPERWORK, THE YOUNG MAN'S ATTENTION IS CAUGHT BY A MOVEMENT ON THE STREET BELOW...

IT'S **ROCHEFORT!** THE DEVIL'S BLOOD, HE WON'T ESCAPE ME **THIS TIME...**

D'ARTAGNAN RUSHES OUT OF THE OFFICE...

...JUST AS ATHOS, RECOVERED FROM HIS FAINTING SPELL, EMERGES INTO THE CORRIDOR...

OOOW!

EXCUSE ME, I'M IN A HURRY!

WAIT A **SECOND**, YOUNG MAN! DO YOU THINK THAT'S A **SUFFICIENT APOLOGY** TO A **MUSKETEER?**

I SAID 'EXCUSE ME' - THAT SEEMS **GOOD** ENOUGH TO ME!

YOU'RE **IMPOLITE**, SIR! I CAN **TELL** YOU'RE FROM THE **COUNTRYSIDE!**

COUNTRY BOY OR NOT, IF I WASN'T IN SUCH A **HURRY**, I'D GIVE *YOU* A LESSON IN **MANNERS...**

YOU WON'T NEED TO **RUN** TO FIND **ME!** SHALL WE MEET, SAY, BY THE **CONVENT OF THE CARMES-DÉSCHAUX,** AT MIDDAY?

VERY WELL! I LOOK FORWARD TO OUR **DUEL.**

DON'T KEEP ME **WAITING,** OR I'LL BE THE ONE RUNNING AFTER **YOU!**

D'ARTAGNAN RACES OUTSIDE, WHERE PORTHOS IS DEEP IN CONVERSATION...

BUT A GUST OF WIND CATCHES THE MUSKETEER'S CLOAK AND...

MMMMFFFH!

THE **DEVIL'S TEETH,** MAN!

YOU MUST BE **INSANE, THROWING** YOURSELF AT PEOPLE LIKE THAT!

EXCUSE ME, I'M RUNNING AFTER SOMEONE AND...

DO YOU FORGET YOUR **EYES** WHEN YOU'RE RUNNING?

I CAN *SEE* THE KIND OF MAN *YOU* ARE, WELL ENOUGH!

YOU'LL EARN YOURSELF A **CLOBBERING** IF YOU **PROVOKE** A MUSKETEER LIKE THIS!

LATER, PERHAPS? WHEN YOU'VE DISPOSED OF THAT **CLOAK**!

VERY WELL! I'LL SEE YOU AT **ONE O'CLOCK**, AT THE **LUXEMBOURG GARDENS**!

D'ARTAGNAN TURNS THE CORNER IN PURSUIT OF ROCHEFORT, BUT...

HE'S **GONE!** HE MUST HAVE DUCKED INTO ONE OF THESE HOUSES.

D'ARTAGNAN WALKS ON, THINKING ABOUT THE TWO DUELS HE'S JUST AGREED TO...

MY **HOTHEADEDNESS** WILL BE THE **DEATH** OF ME. I MUST TRY TO BE MORE **POLITE** IN FUTURE...

...IF I **LIVE** THAT LONG!

AH, THERE'S **ARAMIS!**

HE'S DROPPED HIS **HANDKERCHIEF**...

I BELIEVE THIS IS **YOURS**, SIR? IT WOULD BE A **PITY** TO **LOSE** IT.

D'ARTAGNAN HEARS THE BELL OF A NEARBY CLOCK TOWER STRIKING TWELVE, AND HURRIES TO THE GROUNDS OF THE CONVENT OF THE CARMES-DÉSCHAUX...

...WHERE HE FINDS ATHOS WAITING FOR HIM...

I'VE SENT WORD TO **TWO** OF MY **FRIENDS** TO ACT AS **SECONDS** FOR THE DUEL, BUT THEY'RE NOT HERE YET.

I HAVE **NO SECONDS**, I ONLY ARRIVED IN PARIS **YESTERDAY** AND I KNOW **NO ONE** HERE, EXCEPT MONSIEUR DE TRÉVILLE.

I **DIDN'T** REALIZE. I SHOULD FEEL **ASHAMED** TO FIGHT A **FRIENDLESS** YOUNG BOY!

THERE'S NO NEED FOR **SHAME**, SIR. AFTER ALL, YOU'RE **SUFFERING** FROM A **WOUND** THAT MUST PUT YOU AT A **DISADVANTAGE!**

I CAN FIGHT **EQUALLY WELL** WITH MY **LEFT** HAND...

OW!

...THOUGH IT'S TRUE MY **RIGHT** SHOULDER IS **ON FIRE!**

I HAVE A **BALM** AT MY LODGINGS THAT MY MOTHER GAVE ME WHICH HAS A **MARVELLOUS EFFECT** ON WOUNDS...

...IT TAKES **THREE DAYS** TO WORK, BUT WE COULD RESUME OUR DUEL AFTER THAT?

I'VE BEEN TRYING TO **TRACE** HIM, WITHOUT SUCCESS!

WHY SHOULD HE ABDUCT **YOUR WIFE**?

SHE'S ONE OF THE **FEW** PEOPLE AT THE PALACE WHO'S **LOYAL** TO THE **QUEEN**...

...THE CARDINAL **SPIES** ON THE QUEEN AND THE KING **SHUNS** HER!

A FEW DAYS AGO, MY WIFE TOLD ME THAT THE QUEEN WAS VERY **AFRAID**...

...APPARENTLY THE CARDINAL IS **PERSECUTING** HER MORE THAN EVER!

FOR WHAT **REASON**?

HE BELIEVES THAT THE QUEEN HAS BEEN **SECRETLY COMMUNICATING** WITH A GENTLEMAN IN ENGLAND – **THE DUKE OF BUCKINGHAM!**

AS YOU KNOW, WE'RE ON THE VERGE OF **WAR** WITH THE **ENGLISH.**

THE QUEEN TOLD MY WIFE THAT SHE THINKS A **LETTER** HAS BEEN SENT TO THE DUKE IN THE QUEEN'S NAME, ASKING HIM TO COME TO **PARIS**...

...BUT IT'S REALLY DESIGNED TO **LURE** THE DUKE INTO A **TRAP!**

BUT WHAT DOES YOUR **WIFE** HAVE TO DO WITH ALL THIS?

THE CARDINAL KNOWS HOW **DEVOTED** MY WIFE IS TO THE QUEEN. PERHAPS HE PLANS TO FORCE HER TO **REVEAL** THE QUEEN'S **SECRETS**, OR TO TURN MY WIFE INTO A **SPY**?

THE CARDINAL'S MEN MIGHT COME FOR **ME** NEXT! THIS MORNING I RECEIVED THIS **NOTE**...

Don't go looking for your wife. She will be restored to you when she is no longer needed. If you make any attempt to find her, you are lost.

YOU MUST BE VERY **WORRIED** ABOUT YOUR WIFE.

MY WIFE EARNS A **GOOD WAGE** AT THE PALACE AND I'LL BE **OUT OF POCKET** IF SHE NEVER COMES BACK!

UM, YES, OF COURSE!

AS THE CARDINAL'S GUARDS ARE GREAT RIVALS OF YOUR FRIENDS THE **MUSKETEERS**, I THOUGHT YOU MIGHT ALL ENJOY THE CHANCE TO CAUSE THE CARDINAL SOME **TROUBLE**?

I DARE SAY.

AND AS YOU ALSO OWE ME THREE MONTHS' **RENT**...

AHEM, YES, QUITE...

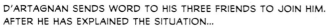

D'ARTAGNAN SENDS WORD TO HIS THREE FRIENDS TO JOIN HIM. AFTER HE HAS EXPLAINED THE SITUATION...

IT COULD TAKE **TIME** TO FIND HER.

THEN WE MUST **HURRY**. MADAME BONACIEUX COULD BE BEING **TORTURED** AS WE SPEAK, SIMPLY FOR BEING **LOYAL** TO HER MISTRESS...

...NOT TO MENTION THE QUEEN **HERSELF**. SHE'S **ABANDONED** BY THE KING AND **PERSECUTED** BY THE CARDINAL!

BUT YOU **SAID** YOU WERE GOING TO...

SSH! WE CAN ONLY HELP YOU IF WE'RE **FREE**. IF WE **DEFEND** YOU **NOW**, THEY'LL **ARREST** US **TOO**!

AFTER MONSIEUR BONACIEUX HAS BEEN TAKEN AWAY...

HOW COULD YOU LET THEM TAKE HIM AWAY WITHOUT A **FIGHT**, D'ARTAGNAN?

DON'T BE A **FOOL**, PORTHOS. D'ARTAGNAN HAS USED HIS **HEAD**!

BUT...

I'LL EXPLAIN TO YOU **LATER**, PORTHOS, OLD FELLOW!

AND NOW, GENTLEMEN... '**ALL FOR ONE, ONE FOR ALL**', THAT IS OUR **MOTTO**, IS IT NOT?

ALL FOR ONE, ONE FOR ALL!

THE MEN ARE NO MATCH FOR D'ARTAGNAN...

AND DON'T COME BACK!

D'ARTAGNAN REMOVES MADAME BONACIEUX'S GAG...

THANK YOU, MONSIEUR D'ARTAGNAN. YOU MAY HAVE SAVED MY **LIFE**!

BUT WHERE'S MY **HUSBAND**?

IMPRISONED IN THE **BASTILLE**, ALAS!

AFTER D'ARTAGNAN HAS RECOUNTED THE EVENTS LEADING TO MONSIEUR BONACIEUX'S ARREST...

MY HUSBAND KNOWS **NOTHING** THAT WILL BE OF ANY **USE** TO THE MEN BEHIND MY ABDUCTION.

WHERE WERE YOU **HELD**, MADAME? AND HOW DID YOU **ESCAPE**?

I WAS **LOCKED** IN THE BEDROOM OF AN **OLD HOUSE** ON THE OTHER SIDE OF THE CITY. TONIGHT I USED MY **BED SHEETS** TO **CLIMB OUT OF A WINDOW**, THEN **RAN** ALL THE WAY HERE!

I ONLY CAME HERE TO SEE MY **HUSBAND**. ONCE I'M **BACK** AT THE **PALACE** I'M SURE THE QUEEN WILL PROTECT ME.

THEN I MUST **ESCORT** YOU!

NO, YOU'VE **ALREADY** RISKED **TOO MUCH** FOR ME, MONSIEUR.

BESIDES, BEFORE THAT, THERE'S AN **IMPORTANT TASK** I WAS DUE TO CARRY OUT TONIGHT.

THEN ALLOW ME TO **ASSIST** YOU IN **THAT**!

YOU'RE VERY **KIND**. BUT THE **FEWER** PEOPLE **INVOLVED**, THE **BETTER**.

MADAME BONACIEUX BIDS D'ARTAGNAN FAREWELL AND HEADS OFF INTO THE NIGHT...

SUCH A **GENTLE** AND **BEAUTIFUL** LADY SHOULD NOT BE EXPOSED TO **FURTHER DANGER**!

AND SO, KEEPING A DISCREET DISTANCE, D'ARTAGNAN FOLLOWS MADAME BONACIEUX THROUGH THE DARKENED STREETS...

MADAME BONACIEUX STOPS AT A HOUSE IN RUE DE LA HARPE...

TAP! TAP! TAP! TAP!

THE DOOR OPENS, AND MOMENTS LATER, A MUSKETEER EMERGES...

THAT LOOKS LIKE **ARAMIS**!

I'VE ONLY SEEN YOU *FOUR* TIMES IN *THREE YEARS*, MADAM, BUT EACH OCCASION FILLED MY HEART WITH **JOY!**

IT'S **MADNESS** TO SPEAK LIKE THIS, MY LORD! YOU REALIZE THAT THE CARDINAL HAS **POISONED** YOUR **REPUTATION** WITH THE KING?

I KNOW. IN MORE PEACEFUL TIMES, HIS MAJESTY **REFUSED** MY REQUEST TO COME HERE AS AN **AMBASSADOR.**

BUT FRANCE WILL **PAY** FOR HER KING'S REFUSAL **WITH WAR!**

SOON I SHALL BE LEADING AN ENGLISH **ARMY** INTO **LA ROCHELLE...**

...AS YOU KNOW, THE PEOPLE THERE WANT TO **REBEL** AGAINST THE KING FOR HIS OPPOSITION TO THEIR RELIGION. I **SHALL HELP THEM!**

WHEN IT'S OVER, **SOMEONE** WILL BE NEEDED TO COME TO PARIS TO MAKE **PEACE.** THAT MAN WILL BE **ME**, AND I'LL BE ABLE TO SEE YOU AGAIN!

BUT WHAT IF YOU'RE **KILLED IN BATTLE?** OH, IF I THOUGHT YOU'D **DIED** FOR **MY LOVE**, I'D **NEVER** FORGIVE MYSELF!

YOU MUST GO NOW, BUT IF YOU **PROMISE** ME YOU'LL KEEP YOURSELF **FREE FROM HARM,** I'LL **GLADLY** SEE YOU AGAIN!

VERY WELL. AS LONG AS YOU **PROMISE** TO **LEAVE** FRANCE NOW AND **RETURN** TO ENGLAND!

I SHALL. BUT GIVE ME A **PLEDGE** OF YOUR **LOVE,** SOMETHING YOU'VE WORN, THAT I CAN WEAR **IN TURN!**

THE QUEEN GOES TO HER CHAMBERS AND RETURNS A FEW MOMENTS LATER...

TAKE THIS SASH ADORNED WITH **TWELVE DIAMONDS,** IN MEMORY OF ME.

NOW **GO!**

MADAME BONACIEUX ESCAPED FROM WHERE I WAS HOLDING HER AND ESCORTED THE DUKE TO THE QUEEN!

WE'LL DEAL WITH THAT DEVIOUS SEAMSTRESS LATER. DO WE KNOW WHAT PASSED BETWEEN THE QUEEN AND THE DUKE?

THE QUEEN PRESENTED HIM WITH THE TWELVE DIAMONDS THAT WERE GIVEN TO HER BY HIS MAJESTY THE KING.

THAT'S GOOD! ALL IS NOT LOST, ROCHEFORT. IN FACT, THINGS MAY HAVE WORKED OUT FOR THE BEST!

IF YOU SAY SO, YOUR EMINENCE, BUT I DON'T SEE HOW...

THE CARDINAL WRITES A LETTER...

Milady,
Be at the next ball the Duke of Buckingham attends.
He will be wearing twelve diamonds. Get close to him and cut off two.
As soon as you have them, bring them to me.
R

HOW I CAN MAKE UP FOR YOUR INCOMPETENCE? YOU'LL SEE...

GET ONE OF OUR AGENTS TO DELIVER THIS TO MILADY IN LONDON!

THAT EVENING, MADAME BONACIEUX IS DISTRESSED TO HEAR HER MISTRESS CRYING...

WHAT'S **WRONG**, YOUR MAJESTY?

THE KING **INSISTS** I WEAR MY **DIAMOND SASH** AT A BALL IN TWO WEEKS' TIME. BUT I'VE **GIVEN** IT TO THE **DUKE!**

I'M **SURE** THE **CARDINAL** IS BEHIND IT. HE MEANS TO **EXPOSE** ME!

THERE'S **STILL TIME** FOR SOMEONE TO GO TO **ENGLAND** AND FETCH THE SASH **BACK!**

BUT WHO CAN WE **TRUST?**

I'LL ASK MY **HUSBAND!**

I THOUGHT HE WAS HELD **PRISONER** IN THE **BASTILLE?**

THE CARDINAL **RELEASED** HIM LAST WEEK.

IT'S **UNUSUAL** FOR THE CARDINAL TO BE SO **LENIENT.** BUT WE MUST BE THANKFUL.

I'LL WRITE A **LETTER** FOR YOUR **HUSBAND** TO GIVE TO THE **DUKE...**

HER **MAJESTY** WANTS YOU TO GO ON A **MISSION** TO ENGLAND!

YOU'RE TO **SEEK OUT** AN **EMINENT** FRIEND OF HERS WHO WILL GIVE YOU AN **ITEM** TO BRING BACK!

I CAN'T GO **RUNNING ERRANDS** FOR THE QUEEN. I PROMISED THE **CARDINAL** I'D WORK ON **HIS** BEHALF FROM NOW ON!

THE **CARDINAL!** WHY YOU **TRAITOR!** SO THAT'S WHY HE LET YOU GO!

YOU SHOULD BE **GRATEFUL.** HE'S PAYING ME **HANDSOMELY!**

PUT THAT MONEY SOMEWHERE **SAFE** WHILE I'M OUT!

I'LL GO AND TELL THE CARDINAL'S FRIEND **MONSIEUR ROCHEFORT** WHAT THE QUEEN'S **UP TO!**

NOW WHAT AM I GOING TO DO?

GOOD EVENING, MADAME!

MONSIEUR D'ARTAGNAN!

I **OVERHEARD** YOUR CONVERSATION. IT SEEMS YOU'RE IN NEED OF A **MESSENGER**?

A GRATEFUL MADAME BONACIEUX GIVES D'ARTAGNAN THE FULL DETAILS OF THE MISSION...

I COULD **NEVER** DO THAT. FOR YOU **MUST KNOW** THAT I HAVE FALLEN IN **LOVE** WITH YOU, CONSTANCE!

...I'VE **ENTRUSTED** YOU WITH **SECRETS**, MONSIEUR. PLEASE DON'T **BETRAY** THAT TRUST.

IT'S TRUE MY **HUSBAND** IS NO LONGER WORTHY OF **THAT TITLE**, BUT YOU ARE **TOO BOLD**, MONSIEUR!

I SHALL **PROVE** MY LOVE FOR YOU BY COMPLETING YOUR TASK!

I HAVE NO **TIME** TO **ARGUE** WITH YOU, MONSIEUR.

NOW THEN, YOU MAY NEED **MONEY**. TAKE **THIS**!

HA HA! IS THIS THE **PAYMENT** YOUR **HUSBAND** SPOKE OF?

IT WILL BE **TWICE** AS ENTERTAINING TO SAVE THE **QUEEN** WITH THE *CARDINAL'S* MONEY!

D'ARTAGNAN VISITS HIS THREE FRIENDS, BEGINNING WITH ATHOS...

IT'S A **DANGEROUS** MISSION FOR THE SAKE OF A FEW **JEWELS!**

BUT THINK OF WHAT WILL HAPPEN TO THE **QUEEN** IF THEY'RE NOT RETURNED.

BESIDES, I GAVE MY WORD TO **MADAME BONACIEUX...**

AH, NOW I THINK I SEE YOUR **TRUE** MOTIVE...

I DON'T KNOW WHAT YOU MEAN.

NEVER TRUST A WOMAN, MY BOY. I **ONCE DID** AND I'VE **REGRETTED** IT EVER SINCE!

WHAT HAPPENED?

WE WERE BOTH **YOUNG.** IT WAS LOVE AT FIRST SIGHT ON MY PART.

I SHARED **EVERYTHING** I HAD WITH HER. THEN, ONE DAY, I FOUND OUT THE **TRUTH...**

WHAT TRUTH?

THAT WAS **FOOLISH** OF YOU, PORTHOS.

BUT THERE'S NO TURNING BACK NOW. **KILL** THIS FELLOW AND **CATCH UP** AS **FAST** AS YOU **CAN**!

I'LL **PERFORATE** YOU WITH EVERY **STRIKE** KNOWN IN FENCING!

AS THE OTHERS GO ON THEIR WAY...

I'M GUESSING THAT MAN WAS HIRED TO **DELAY** US. BUT WHY DO YOU SUPPOSE HE PICKED ON **PORTHOS**?

PORTHOS HAS THE **LOUDEST VOICE** OF ALL OF US. THAT FELLOW MUST HAVE **ASSUMED** HE WAS OUR **LEADER**!

AT BEAUVAIS, THE FRIENDS STOP AND WAIT FOR PORTHOS TO CATCH UP. BUT AFTER WAITING FOR TWO HOURS, THEY ARE FORCED TO CARRY ON WITHOUT HIM.

THEY ARE PASSING A GROUP OF ROAD WORKERS, WHEN...

BANG!

WHEN THEY ARRIVE, THE DUKE SHOWS D'ARTAGNAN INTO HIS PRIVATE CHAPEL...

I KEEP THE DIAMOND SASH IN HERE!

BUT WHEN THE DUKE OPENS THE BOX CONTAINING THE SASH...

TWO OF THE DIAMONDS ARE **MISSING!** THERE ARE ONLY **TEN** LEFT!

WHO COULD HAVE **STOLEN** THEM?

THE ONLY TIME THEY'VE BEEN OUT OF HERE WAS WHEN I WORE THEM AT THE **KING'S BALL** AT WINDSOR...

OF COURSE! **LADY DE WINTER** MUST HAVE TAKEN THEM! I **FELL OUT** WITH HER SOME TIME AGO, BUT **THAT NIGHT** SHE **INSISTED** ON KEEPING **CLOSE** TO ME!

NOW YOU KNOW **WHY!**

OUR ONLY HOPE IS TO GET **REPLACEMENTS** MADE. I'LL SET MY PERSONAL GOLDSMITH ONTO IT **AT ONCE!**

TWO DAYS LATER, THE WORK IS DONE...

THE **BALL** IS **TOMORROW NIGHT**. SO YOU **MUST** GET THESE BACK TO THE QUEEN BY THEN*!*

A **SHIP** IS WAITING FOR YOU ON THE **THAMES**.

D'ARTAGNAN UNDERTAKES A BREAKNECK, HEART-POUNDING JOURNEY AND EVENTUALLY ARRIVES IN PARIS LESS THAN AN HOUR BEFORE THE BALL...

TWENTY MINUTES LATER, THE KING IS ON HIS WAY TO THE PALACE BALLROOM WHEN HE IS APPROACHED BY THE CARDINAL...

YOU MAY BE **INTERESTED** IN THE **CONTENTS** OF THIS **BOX** YOUR MAJESTY.

TWO DIAMONDS? WHAT DOES THIS **MEAN?**

I DOUBT THE QUEEN WILL BE WEARING HER **DIAMOND SASH** TONIGHT, SIRE*!*

AND EVEN IF SHE **IS**, YOU WILL ONLY COUNT *TEN* JEWELS. ASK HER WHAT HAPPENED TO THE OTHER **TWO***!*

THERE WAS A **TALL, THIN, DARK-HAIRED** GENTLEMAN WITH A **SCAR**, AND A **SHORT, PLUMP, OLDER** MAN WITH A **SMALL, POINTED BEARD.**

ROCHEFORT! THE OTHER FELLOW SOUNDS **FAMILIAR** TOO!

DID YOU SEE A **LADY?**

YES SIR. AFTER THE SHORT MAN WENT IN BY THE DOOR, THERE WERE **SHOUTS** FROM INSIDE, AND I HEARD A SCUFFLE...

...THEN A **LADY** APPEARED AT THE **WINDOW** WITH A **TERRIFIED** LOOK UPON HER FACE. THE TALL GENTLEMAN'S SERVANT WAS ALREADY ON THE LADDER, **BLOCKING** HER **ESCAPE**...

...HE **CARRIED** THE LADY **DOWN** THE **LADDER** AND INTO THE CARRIAGE. THE SHORT MAN AND THE OTHER GENTLEMAN JOINED THEM AND THEY **RODE OFF!**

D'ARTAGNAN LEAPS ONTO HIS HORSE AND GALLOPS BACK TO CENTRAL PARIS...

POOR CONSTANCE HAS BEEN ABDUCTED **AGAIN!** I MUST SEE IF MONSIEUR DE TRÉVILLE CAN HELP!

HO THERE! STOP!

...BUT THE CARRIAGE RATTLES PAST.

THAT EVENING, AT A BACKSTREET TAVERN, D'ARTAGNAN TELLS HIS FRIENDS ABOUT THE INCIDENT...

ARE YOU SURE IT WAS HER?

OF COURSE I'M SURE!

AT LEAST IT PROVES SHE'S ALIVE!

WHERE'S ATHOS? HE'S LATE!

AS ATHOS APPROACHES THE TAVERN, HE SEES A HOODED FIGURE ENTERING AHEAD OF HIM...

CARDINAL RICHELIEU! WHAT'S HE DOING HERE?

THE CARDINAL APPROACHES THE LANDLORD...

I HAVE AN APPOINTMENT IN YOUR UPSTAIRS ROOM.

YES, MONSIEUR. THE LADY TOLD ME TO EXPECT YOU. GO STRAIGHT UP!

HE'LL **NEVER** AGREE!

THEN YOU MUST ARRANGE HIS **ASSASSINATION!**

IF IT BECAME KNOWN I'D BEEN INVOLVED IN THE **MURDER** OF AN **ENGLISH NOBLEMAN**, I COULD FIND MYSELF ON THE **GALLOWS, EVEN** HERE IN FRANCE!

TAKE THIS **OFFICIAL ORDER.** IT STATES THAT **ANY ACTION** TAKEN BY THE HOLDER WAS FOR THE **GOOD OF FRANCE. EVEN** *I* COULDN'T HAVE YOU ARRESTED THEN!

IN THAT CASE, NOT ONLY WILL I HAVE THE DUKE **DISPOSED** OF, BUT ALSO THAT **INTERFERING PUPPY** D'ARTAGNAN!

I ONLY WISH I COULD ALSO GET MY REVENGE ON HIS ACCOMPLICE, **MADAME BONACIEUX!**

I THOUGHT **ROCHEFORT ABDUCTED** HER FROM THE SAINT-CLOUD PAVILION AND **IMPRISONED** HER?

DIDN'T HE TELL YOU? THE **QUEEN** FOUND OUT WHERE SHE WAS BEING HELD AND HAD HER **MOVED** TO A **CONVENT.** WE'VE BEEN UNABLE TO DISCOVER WHICH ONE.

GOOD MORNING, LADY DE WINTER, OR SHOULD I SAY **MILADY**?

BUCKINGHAM!

ALLOW ME TO INTRODUCE YOU TO THE **SLYEST**, **CRUELLEST**, MOST **DECEITFUL** WOMAN ON EITHER SIDE OF THE CHANNEL, FELTON!

YOU **WRONG** ME, SIR!

I WOULD'VE THOUGHT YOU'D BE **FLATTERED**, MILADY!

WHAT GIVES YOU THE **RIGHT** TO HOLD ME **PRISONER**?

I RECEIVED A **WARNING** FROM SOME GALLANT **FRENCH FRIENDS** OF MINE THAT YOU WERE COMING TO ENGLAND TO DO ME **HARM**!

BUT ATHOS SWORE...

WHAT WAS **THAT**, MADAM?

NOTHING.

HOW **LONG** AM I TO BE **KEPT** HERE?

NOT LONG, DON'T WORRY. IN A FEW DAYS TIME, YOU'LL BE ON A SHIP BOUND FOR THE **COLONIES...**

...NEVER TO RETURN!

WATCH HER LIKE A **HAWK,** FELTON. ABOVE ALL, DON'T TRUST HER AN **INCH!**

AS THE DOOR SLAMS SHUT...

I MUST GET OUT OF HERE **QUICKLY.** ONCE I'M STUCK ON A COLONY SHIP, ESCAPE WILL BE **IMPOSSIBLE!**

I'LL NEED **HELP,** BUT I THINK **FELTON** COULD EASILY BE **CONVERTED** BY A SUITABLE **SOB STORY!**

AND SO, WHEN FELTON BRINGS MILADY SOME FOOD...

YOU SEEM A **KIND** MAN, JOHN. HOW CAN YOU BEAR TO SERVE A **MONSTER** LIKE THE DUKE?

HIS GRACE IS **NO MONSTER,** MY LADY.

YOU THINK **NOT**? HE HAS ME LOCKED UP BECAUSE HE'S **AFRAID** OF WHAT I MIGHT **TELL** THE **KING** ABOUT HIM!

I DON'T KNOW WHAT YOU **MEAN**, MY LADY.

MANY YEARS AGO, THE DUKE WANTED ME TO BE HIS **LOVER**.

WHEN I **REFUSED**, HE **BEAT** ME. HE MIGHT HAVE **KILLED** ME IF I HADN'T **RUN AWAY**!

THAT DOESN'T SOUND LIKE THE DUKE *I* KNOW.

HE'S A **CUNNING FOX** WHO'S COVERED HIS TRACKS.

I'M JUST A **WEAK**, **VULNERABLE** WOMAN TO MEN LIKE HIM.

PLEASE **LEAVE ME** NOW. TALKING ABOUT MY **WRETCHED** PAST UPSETS ME!

AS FELTON LEAVES...

HA! I CAN SEE THE FIRST GLIMMERS OF **DOUBT** ABOUT THE DUKE'S **MOTIVES** IN FELTON'S EYES.

A FEW MORE TALES OF **HARDSHIP** AND HE'LL DO **ANYTHING** TO HELP ME!

OVER THE NEXT FEW DAYS, MILADY'S LIES ABOUT THE DUKE'S CRUELTY MAKE FELTON FALL IN LOVE...

HOLD ON **TIGHT!**

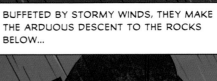

BUFFETED BY STORMY WINDS, THEY MAKE THE ARDUOUS DESCENT TO THE ROCKS BELOW...

...WHERE A SMALL BOAT IS WAITING...

...TO CONVEY THEM TO A LARGER VESSEL...

THE DUKE'S AIDES RUSH IN...

HIS GRACE IS **DEAD!**

SEIZE FELTON!

A CANNON FIRES FROM THE ADMIRALTY TO SIGNAL AN EMERGENCY. LATER, AS FELTON IS LED AWAY...

MILADY'S SHIP! SHE'S **SET SAIL** FOR FRANCE WITHOUT **WAITING** FOR **ME!**

WHEN MILADY ARRIVES IN CALAIS...

IF FELTON **TALKS,** THE ENGLISH AUTHORITIES MAY COME LOOKING FOR ME.

I'D BEST GO INTO **HIDING** SOMEWHERE **SAFE** UNTIL THINGS **CALM DOWN.**

PAUSING TO TAKE REFRESHMENT AT A DOCKSIDE TAVERN, SHE WRITES A NOTE TO THE CARDINAL...

The deed is done. You may contact me at the convent at Béthune.

Milady

YOU BOY! SEE THIS LETTER GETS TO **PARIS!**

MILADY TRAVELS TO BÉTHUNE, WHERE SHE PLEADS WITH THE ABBESS OF THE LOCAL CONVENT TO GRANT HER SANCTUARY...

YOU **POOR** CHILD. PLEASE COME IN.

I HAVE BEEN PERSECUTED BY A **CRUEL** AND **POWERFUL** MAN, AND I **FEAR** FOR MY **SAFETY**!

AFTER THE ABBESS HAS ALLOCATED MILADY A SIMPLE ROOM...

WE HAVE A RECENT ARRIVAL WHO HAS **ALSO** BEEN **ILL-TREATED** BY THOSE IN POWER, MY LADY.

I WILL **INTRODUCE** YOU TO HER. YOU MAY FIND **COMFORT** IN **SHARING** YOUR EXPERIENCES.

A SHORT WHILE LATER, THE ABBESS RETURNS...

MY LADY, THIS IS **CONSTANCE**.

CONSTANCE!? SURELY IT **CAN'T** BE...

COULD YOU PERHAPS BE **MADAME BONACIEUX**?

WHY **YES**. DO YOU **KNOW** ME, MY LADY?

UM, I THINK WE HAVE A MUTUAL FRIEND - **MONSIEUR D'ARTAGNAN**?

MONSIEUR D'ARTAGNAN IS MOST **DEAR** TO ME!

...SO, YOU SEE, MADAME BONACIEUX **HASN'T** ESCAPED US **AFTER ALL!**

AND **D'ARTAGNAN** IS DUE. YOU MUST ARREST THEM **BOTH!**

YES. BUT I'LL **STILL** NEED **AUTHORITY** FROM THE **CARDINAL** TO ARREST A *KING'S GUARD!*

THEN **GET** IT! AND **QUICKLY!**

VERY WELL. BUT THE CARDINAL ORDERED YOU TO MOVE SOMEWHERE MORE **REMOTE**. HERE'S THE ADDRESS...

...IT'S AN **ISOLATED COTTAGE** LESS THAN AN HOUR'S RIDE FROM HERE.

Maison Grise
Avenue des Saules
Armentières

I'LL TAKE THE BONACIEUX WOMAN **THERE** IF D'ARTAGNAN ARRIVES **BEFORE** YOU RETURN!

THAT EVENING, OVER SUPPER, CONSTANCE TELLS MILADY WHAT SHE'S BEEN THROUGH...

AFTER WHAT YOU'VE TOLD ME, PERHAPS YOU SHOULD BE **WARY** OF THE **LETTER** YOU RECEIVED?

IT COULD BE A **FAKE**, INTENDED TO **KEEP** YOU **HERE** UNTIL THE CARDINAL'S MEN ARRIVE TO **ARREST** YOU.

I KNOW A **COTTAGE NEARBY** WHERE I COULD TAKE YOU FOR **SAFETY**. THE ABBESS COULD SEND WORD IF D'ARTAGNAN ARRIVES **HERE**.

AN ADDRESS IN **ARMENTIÈRES!**

THAT'S OUR BEST CHANCE. **LET'S GO!**

BEFORE THEY LEAVE, D'ARTAGNAN EXPLAINS TO THE ABBESS WHAT HAS HAPPENED...

...I SHALL RETURN **SOON** TO PAY MY **LAST RESPECTS** TO CONSTANCE.

GOD BE WITH YOU, MY SON!

THE FOUR MEN RACE NORTHWARDS...

AN HOUR LATER, THEY ARRIVE AT THEIR DESTINATION...

WELL *SOMEONE'S* THERE. I SEE A **LIGHT!**

I'LL TAKE THE **WINDOW.** YOU GUARD THE **DOOR!**

GASP!

EVEN THOUGH SHE PRETENDS TO BE ENGLISH, AS SOON AS I HEARD HER **VOICE** THROUGH THAT **STOVE PIPE**, I **KNEW** IT WAS HER!

WHY DIDN'T YOU **SAY** SO?

BECAUSE WHILE ONLY *I* KNEW SHE WAS A **BRANDED CRIMINAL**, I HAD A **HOLD** OVER HER.

I DID WHAT YOU WANTED, DIDN'T I?

I WENT BACK TO THE TAVERN AND TOLD HER THAT I'D **REVEAL** HER **CRIMINAL PAST** AND **RUIN** HER, UNLESS SHE AGREED TO **DROP** HER PLAN TO HAVE D'ARTAGNAN **KILLED**.

WHAT ABOUT **BUCKINGHAM**?

I DARED NOT **OVERPLAY** MY HAND. THE BEST WE COULD DO WAS TO **WARN** HIM.

THOUGH I SWORE TO MILADY THAT I **WOULDN'T**.

I MADE A **MISTAKE** IN **SPARING** HER LIFE THAT NIGHT. BUT I'M SURE THE **PARIS EXECUTIONER** WON'T BE SO LENIENT!

THE **SO-CALLED** LADY DE WINTER, I CHARGE YOU WITH **KIDNAPPING, THEFT** AND **MURDER**!

OH MERCY! MERCY! FORGIVE ME!

YOU SHOWED **NO MERCY** TO POOR **CONSTANCE**!

THEN AT LEAST LET ME HAVE ONE LAST **DRINK**...

NO!

I DIDN'T GIVE THE LATE MADAME BONACIEUX MY **WHOLE** SUPPLY OF **POISON**...

...BETTER **THIS**... THAN AN EXECUTIONER'S... **BLADE!**

MAY THERE BE **MERCY** ON HER SOUL!

The Story of
The Three Musketeers

In the 17th century, the countries of Europe were ruled by kings and queens who required large armies to defend not only their kingdoms but themselves. These armies were divided into many different ranks of soldiers and guards.

A Musketeer of the Guard

A musketeer was a soldier armed with a musket, a long, rifle-like gun that used either gunpowder or bullets, often with a blade called a bayonet which was attached to the muzzle.

In France, the Musketeers of the Guard were created by King Louis XIII in 1622, as a junior unit of the army of the Royal Household. The Musketeers fought either on foot or on horseback.

Not long afterwards, Cardinal Richelieu, Louis' powerful Chief Minister, formed a unit of Musketeers to act as his personal bodyguard. A fierce rivalry soon developed between the King's Musketeers and those of the Cardinal.

This rivalry forms part of the plot of *The Three Musketeers*, written by Alexandre Dumas in 1844.

Dumas was born Dumas Davy de la Pailleterie, in Picardy, France, in 1802. His father had been a general in the French army, though he died when Dumas was only four years old. By the time he moved to Paris in 1822, Dumas had adopted his father's first name, Alexandre, and soon began using Dumas as his last name.

Dumas was working as a junior clerk at the Palais Royal (which had formerly been the residence of Cardinal Richelieu) when he began writing plays. His first play, *Henry III and His Court*, was performed in 1829 and was a great success.

Alexandre Dumas

Further plays were equally well received and he was soon able to take up writing as a full-time job. His career as a novelist began when he adapted his play *Le Capitaine Paul* into a serialized novel in a newspaper.

D'Artagnan

The Three Musketeers, his most famous novel, was first published as a serial in *Le Siècle* magazine between March and July 1844. Dumas based the lead character of d'Artagnan on a man named Charles de Batz-Castelmore d'Artagnan (c. 1611–1673), who was a real-life captain of the Musketeers. The story is a mixture of fictionalized and historical events.

As well as the kings and queens, many of the characters really existed. The Duke of Buckingham was an English naval commander whose campaigns often ended badly. He remained close to King James I of England and his successor Charles I, but his affair with the queen of France is a creation by Dumas. He died when he was stabbed to death in August 1628 at the Greyhound pub in Portsmouth. The assassin was John Felton, an officer who had been wounded during one of Buckingham's campaigns and believed he had been unfairly denied promotion.

The novel was popular enough to warrant several sequels: *Twenty Years After*, published in 1845, which tells the story of the Musketeers' attempts to protect Louis XIV of France and Charles I of England from their enemies, and *The Vicomte of Bragelonne*, serialized from 1847 to 1850. This novel was so long that it was later divided into three, or sometimes four, volumes. The final volume in both cases was entitled *The Man in the Iron Mask*. Along with a later novel, *The Count of Monte Cristo* (1844-1846), this would soon rival *The Three Musketeers* in popularity.

Dumas wrote all the Musketeer stories, which became known as *The d'Artagnan Romances*, in collaboration with a French author named Auguste Maquet (1813-1888), who supplied outlines of the plots and historical research. As well as plays and novels, Dumas wrote numerous magazine and newspaper articles and many works on travel. He died in December 1870 at the age of 68.

The story of *The Three Musketeers* has spawned numerous adaptations. One of the earliest was an opera staged in 1872, for which Dumas himself wrote the words. Since 1903, there have been over twenty film versions, including a silent movie of 1921 starring Douglas Fairbanks, and *The Three Musketeers* (1973) and its sequel *The Four Musketeers* (1974). A 3D movie version was released in 2011.

On television, there have been three BBC adaptations, most recently in 2014 with a series entitled *The Musketeers*.

The Three Musketeers remains one of the most popular historical romances ever told. Their famous cry of, 'All for one, one for all,' may well ring out forever.

The Three Musketeers

Russell Punter was born in Bedfordshire, England. From an early age he enjoyed writing and illustrating his own stories. He trained as a graphic designer at art college in West Sussex before entering publishing in 1987. He has written over sixty books for children, ranging from original stories to adaptations of classic novels.

Matteo Pincelli was born in Bergamo, Italy. He studied anatomy and comics drawing in Bologna and later formed an animation studio together with eight colleagues. He has also worked in France with a production company based in Paris, and has lived in Berlin, Germany, and Milan, Italy. Today he is based in Fano in the Marche region of Italy, where he occupies himself mainly with work as a storyboard artist, television cartoonist and illustrator of children's books.

Mike Collins has been creating comics for over 25 years. Starting on *Spider-Man* and *Transformers* for Marvel UK, he has also worked for DC, 2000AD and a host of other publishers. In that time he's written or drawn almost all the major characters for each company – *Wonder Woman, Batman, Superman, Flash, Teen Titans, X-Men, Captain Britain, Judge Dredd, Sláine, Rogue Trooper, Darkstars, Peter Cannon: Thunderbolt* and more. He currently draws a series of noir crime fiction graphic novels, *Varg Veum*. He also provides storyboards for TV and movies, including *Doctor Who, Sherlock, Igam Ogam, Claude, Hana's Helpline* and *Horrid Henry*.

Cover design: Matt Preston

First published in 2019 by Usborne Publishing Ltd.,
Usborne House, 83-85 Saffron Hill, London EC1N 8RT, England. www.usborne.com
Copyright © 2019 Usborne Publishing Ltd.